Pepper
gets a ne

Budgie, I'm Pepper.
Will you sing for me?

Yes, Pepper, he will.
But give Budgie some
time. He's new here.
Let me give him some
water.

I'll give him
water, Mama.

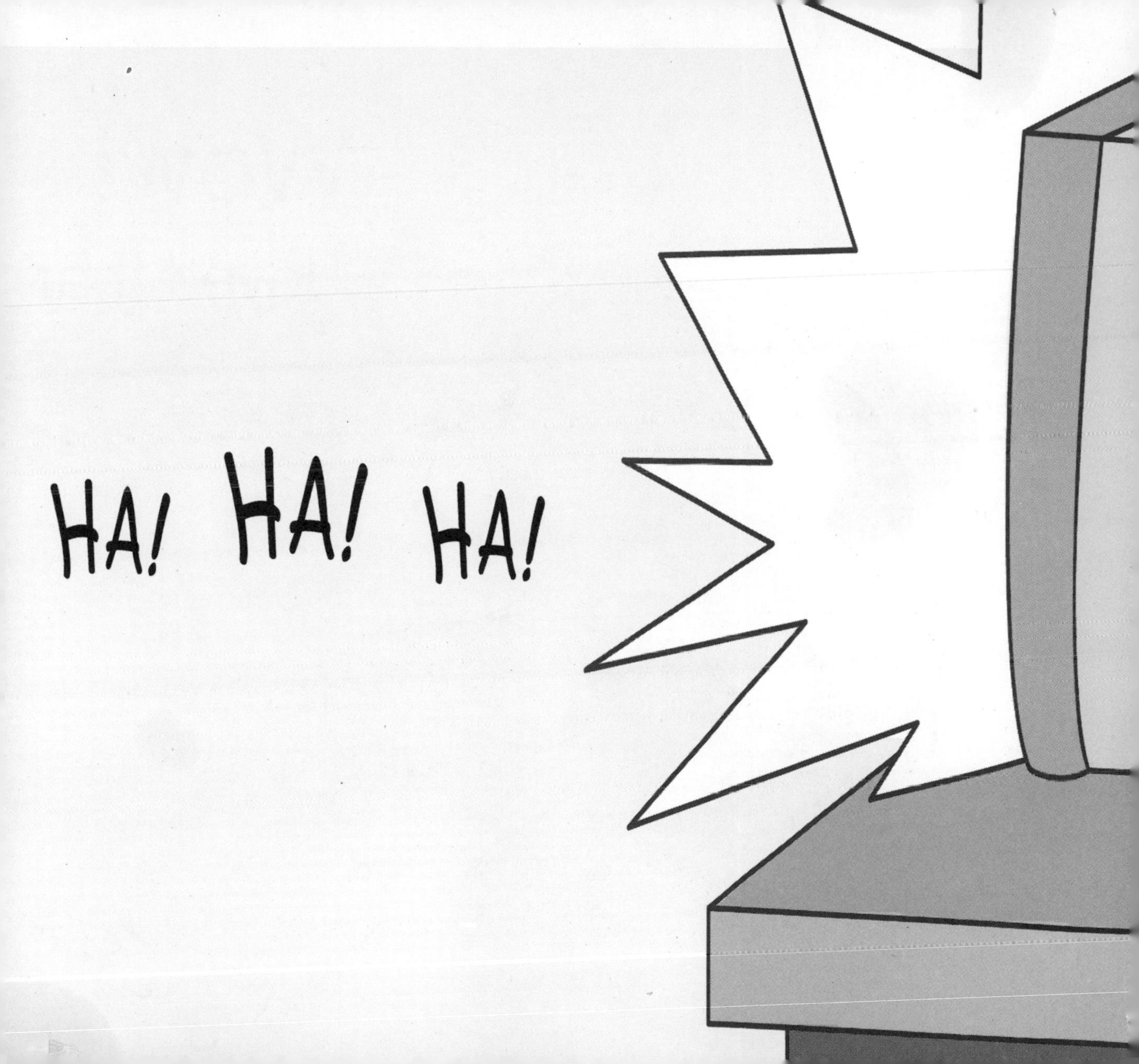
HA! HA! HA!

Wow!

I loved that.

What's the matter?
Oh — oh dear!

Stop crying, Pepper! Budgie is just hot and thirsty. Let's give him some water.

Pepper, I wonder why Budgie's dish is dry. You gave him water, didn't you?

No, Mama.
I ... I went off
to watch TV.

Mama, will Budgie die?

No, Pepper. But when we have a pet, we must take good care of him.

Yes, Mama